$15.00

E   Rylant, Cynthia
RYL   Henry and Mudge and
        the long weekend : the
        eleventh book of their

HENRY AND MUDGE
AND THE
Long Weekend

The Eleventh Book of Their Adventures

Story by Cynthia Rylant
Pictures by Suçie Stevenson

SIMON & SCHUSTER BOOKS FOR YOUNG READERS

For Stephanie, the newest Rylant—CR

For Peter Stevenson and Naomi King—SS

SIMON & SCHUSTER BOOKS FOR YOUNG READERS
An imprint of Simon & Schuster Children's Publishing Division
1230 Avenue of the Americas
New York, New York 10020
Text copyright © 1992 by Cynthia Rylant
llustrations copyright © 1992 by Suçie Stevenson
SIMON & SCHUSTER BOOKS FOR YOUNG READERS is a trademark of Simon & Schuster.

The text of this book was set in 18-point Goudy
The illustrations were rendered in pen-and-ink and watercolor, reproduced in full color.
Series designed by Mina Greenstein
Printed and bound in the United States of America

10 9 8 7 6 5 4 3 2

The Library of Congress has cataloged the hardcover edition as follows:
Rylant, Cynthia.
Henry and Mudge and the long weekend: the eleventh book of their
adventures / story by Cynthia Rylant; pictures by Suçie Stevenson.
p.   cm. (The Henry and Mudge books)
Summary: Henry and Mudge the dog's boring weekend becomes
interesting when Mom suggests building a castle in the basement.
[1. Dogs—Fiction. 2.Play—Fiction.] I. Stevenson, Suçie, ill.
II. Title.   III. Series: Rylant, Cynthia. Henry and Mudge books.
PZ7.R982Hg 1992
[E]-dc20   90-26799
ISBN 0-689-81009-1 (hc) 0-689-80885-2 (pbk)

Contents

Wet Yuck

Henry and Henry's big dog Mudge
woke up one Saturday in February
and looked outside.
"Yuck," said Henry.
It was gray.
It was cold.
It was muddy and wet.

5

"No sun," Henry said.

"No snow.

Just yuck. Wet yuck."

Mudge leaned against Henry and drooled.

"What are we going to do all

weekend?" Henry asked.

Mudge leaned harder.

"How will we have some fun?"

Henry grumbled.

Mudge leaned harder still.

"What a boring weekend,"
Henry growled.

Mudge let go and leaned all the way.

"Whoa!" yelled Henry.

Mudge flattened Henry like a pancake.

"How are we going to get *up*?"
Henry wondered.

Bored

Henry and Mudge had a boring breakfast.

They watched some boring cartoons.

They listened to Henry's father

tell some boring jokes.

"Boy, is this boring," said Henry.

"What are we going to *do?*" he asked.

Mudge knew what to do.

Mudge always knew what to do
if there was nothing interesting to eat,
nothing interesting to smell,
and nothing interesting to chew.
He went to sleep.
"No, Mudge," said Henry,
giving him a push.
"Wake up."

"Pre-spring meanies?"

"Okay, Dad, okay!" Henry sa[id.]

"Boy, are you bored!" said H[enry.]

The three of them sat.

Their eyes kept closing,

their heads kept nodding,

and one of their mouths kept [drooling.]

Henry's mother saw them.

"Goodness," she said. "This [is]

a long weekend."

Then she had an idea.

Mudge sat up.

He wanted to stay awake.

He tried to stay awake.

But everything was so boring

that he couldn't.

His eyes kept closing.

His head kept nodding.

His mouth kept drooling.

"Exciting dog you have th
said Henry's father.
"He's bored," said Henry
"Mudge is bored. I'm bor
Boy, is this boring."
Henry's father frowned.
"February cranks?" he asl
Henry nodded.
"Winter grumpies?"
Henry nodded again.

The Idea

"I have an idea," Henry's mother said.

Henry opened his eyes.

Henry's father sat up.

But Mudge kept on sleeping.

He didn't care much about ideas.

Not until the ideas smelled like something.

"Let's make a castle," said Henry's mother.

"A castle?" said Henry and Henry's father.

"We still have the box the new
refrigerator came in,
and the box the new stove came in."

Henry was getting the idea.

"And that paint set Uncle Arthur
gave me," said Henry.

"Let's do it!"

They headed for the basement.

Mudge was still trying to sleep.

But when he heard voices in the

basement, he woke up fast.

Mudge loved the basement.

It had millions of new smells.

It had lots of places to hide.

And some of his old dog toys

were down there.

"Come on, Mudge!" Henry called.

But Mudge was already on his way.

Down in the Basement

"It has to have turrets," Henry's father said.

"And a drawbridge. And buttresses. And flags."

"Dad," said Henry, "it's just

a refrigerator box."

"Not for long," said Henry's father.

Henry ran upstairs for his castle book.

Henry's mother ran upstairs for pencils.

Henry's father ran upstairs for a stapler.

And Mudge ran upstairs for a quick snack.

They all looked at each other in the kitchen.
"How'd we all get up here again?" asked
Henry's father.

When they got back to the basement,
Henry opened up his castle book.
"Let's make this one," he said.
Henry's father took a look.
Henry's mother took a look.
"Okay," they said.

One of them drew,
one of them cut,
one of them stapled.

And one of them went looking for
an old boot he used to chew.
They all worked a long time
until somebody said,
"Is anyone hungry?"
"Order a pizza," said Henry's father.
"We can't stop now!"
They worked awhile longer
until the pizza came.

Then they stopped and ate pizza
while they stared at the castle
they were building.
They each imagined how it
would look when it was done.

For the rest of the afternoon
they cut out fancy windows
and fancy doors.
They cut out turrets and buttresses
and flags.
Mudge chewed his old boot like crazy.

When evening came and Henry finally
had to crawl into bed,
he could hardly wait to finish the castle.
He could hardly wait
for more of the long weekend.

A Great Weekend

Henry woke up. He looked outside.

"Wet yuck," he said.

But he didn't care.

"We have a castle to finish,"

he told Mudge.

Henry and Henry's father ate some

cold cereal and ran to the basement.

Henry's mother stayed in the kitchen
to read the morning paper.
She was always better at thinking up
ideas than at finishing them.
"Besides," she said, "you have to have
somebody to surprise."

Henry and Henry's father painted
the castle all morning.

While they worked Mudge sniffed
screwdrivers and paint cans
and dirty rags
and beach balls
and Christmas decorations
and a stuffed turkey.

He also tried to eat a spider
but he missed.

Henry and Henry's father

were very quiet.

They wanted to pay attention.

They wanted to do a good job.

Every now and then Henry's mother

would call out,

"Is there life down there?"

Finally, close to lunchtime,

Henry looked at his father.

His father looked at him.

"Wow," they both said.

"Come look! Come look!"

they called up the stairs.

Henry's mother went to the top of
the stairs.
"Not yet! Not yet!" they called.
She waited.

"Okay! Okay!" they called.

She went down the stairs

and there she saw the most beautiful castle

and the most beautiful knights

and the most beautiful king she'd ever seen.

They all spent a long time admiring

the castle.

They took turns sitting in it.

They stuck their heads through its windows.

They opened and closed its doors.

They lowered its drawbridge over and over.

Henry was thrilled.

He gave his parents a big hug.

He gave Mudge a big hug.

"What a weekend," said Henry.

The king gave him a big lick.

"And what a great king!"